BILLY THE GREAT

Rosa Guy

illustrated by
Caroline Binch

DELACORTE PRESS · NEW YORK

For Otonia
R G

For Sam and Sybil
C B

Published by
Delacorte Press
Bantam Doubleday Dell Publishing Group, Inc.
666 Fifth Avenue
New York, New York 10103

This book was originally published in Great Britain in 1991 by Victor Gollancz Ltd.

Library of Congress Cataloging-in-Publication Data
Guy, Rosa.
Billy the Great / Rosa Guy ; illustrated by Caroline Binch.
p.   cm.
Summary: Billy's parents try to plan his life for him, including his choice of friends,
but he has ideas of his own.
ISBN 0-385-30666-0
[1. Individuality—Fiction. 2. Parent and child—Fiction.
3. Friendship—Fiction. 4. Afro-Americans—Fiction.]
I. Binch, Caroline, ill. II. Title.
PZ7.G987Bi 1992
[E]—dc20   91-34704
                                                      CIP
                                                      AC

Manufactured in Singapore
September 1992

10 9 8 7 6 5 4 3 2 1

"What a bright little baby," Billy's mother said
the day he was born. Billy's father agreed.

Later, when Billy turned his head to look around,
his father said, "See his fine, strong back."

Billy kicked his legs and grinned.

When Billy was one year old, Mom said, "My Billy is going to be a great man."

Dad said, "Let's give him time to grow a little."

Billy just laughed.

When Billy was four, his mother said, "We have
to get Billy ready for college."
  "Let's get him through grade school first," Dad said.
  Billy smiled.

"My Billy is going to be a teacher," Mom said when she saw him teaching his teddy bears the ABCs just the way she had taught Billy. "He might even be a university professor."

"What?" Dad said. "Shut him up in a classroom? With his strong back and legs? No, Billy's going to be a great soccer player."

One day Billy bandaged his dog from head to paws, except for his nose. Mom said, "How intelligent. Billy left room for Rover to breathe. My Billy's going to be a doctor."

She bought Billy a stethoscope and more bandages.
But Rover refused to let Billy practice on him again.

When Billy was six, Rodney moved in next door. Rodney's father was a truck driver. He was a big man, with broad shoulders and thick, tattooed arms. Billy liked Rodney.

"How ya doing, kid," Rodney said, looking down at Billy.

"My name is Rodney, but call me Rod."

That made Billy feel grown-up. "How ya doing, Rod," he said.

"Come over for a snack later," Rod said.

Billy went. He tried to keep up with Rod, eating piece after piece of pie.

"I don't want to play with *children*," Billy said. "I want to play with Rod."

Mom said, "Play with children your own age."

"I'll get dirty," Billy said.

"A little dirt won't matter," Mom said.

Billy went to play with children his own age. They made
mud pies and threw them at him.

Mud went all over Billy.

Billy threw mud pies back.

Mud got into Jeanie's hair and she ran home crying.

She brought her mom over to Billy's house.
   "Billy's sorry," Mom told Jeanie's mother.
   "Billy, tell Jeanie you won't do it again."
   "She started it," Billy said.
   "Now, Billy," Mom said, "tell Jeanie you're sorry."
   Billy refused. He wasn't sorry.

Then Mom scolded him. "How did you get so dirty?" she said. "How did you get mud in your hair?"
She scrubbed hard to get him clean. It hurt.

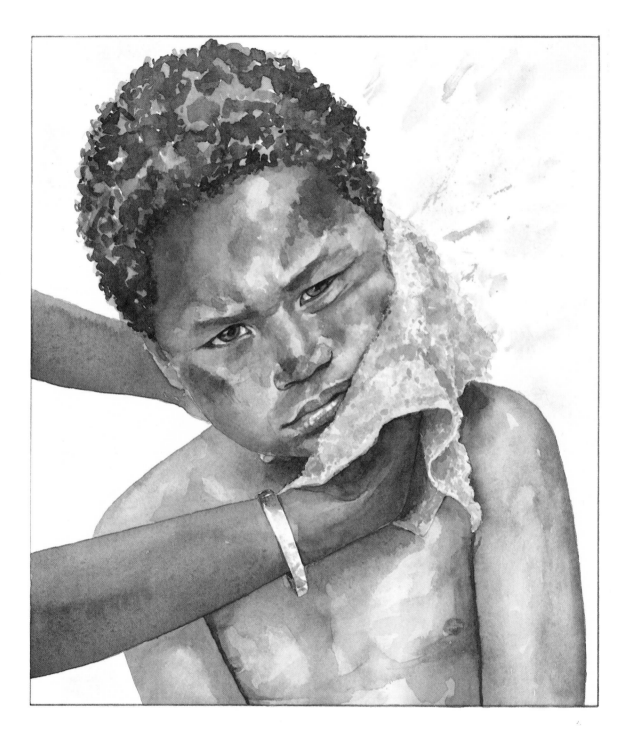

On Billy's seventh birthday Dad bought Billy a big leather soccer ball.

"Now we can start training you to be a great soccer player," Dad said.

Dad took Billy into the backyard. "Stand there and watch, Billy," he said. "First I'll show you the proper way to kick the ball."

Billy stood and watched. Dad kicked the ball. It flew through the air and bounced off the tree.

The ball flew and flew, and flew right through the glass of Rod's window.

Rod's father came out. He shouted at Dad. Rod's father was big and broad, and he had tattoos.

"Don't shout at me," Dad said.

Then Rod came out.

"How ya doing, kid," Rod said.
   "How ya doing, Rod," Billy said.
   "I can do handstands and cartwheels,"
Rod said. "Can you?"
   "I think I can," Billy said.

Rod stood on his hands, feet in the air. Then he flipped over on one hand, then onto his feet,

then back on his other hand, just like a wheel.
Billy tried and tried.

On his third try he stood on his hands, his feet in the air.
He flipped over on one hand, then stood up. He had done it!
   "Billy!" Mom called from the kitchen. She sounded angry.
Then she saw Rod's father eyeballing Billy's father.
   "He broke my window," Rod's father said.
   "Did you tell him we'd fix it?" Mom said.
   "He shouted at me," Dad said.

"Mom," Billy said, "Rod showed me how to do a handstand—watch!" Once again Billy stood on his hands, his feet straight up and steady over his head.

Mom stared. . . .

"Did you call me for something, Mom?" Billy asked.
   She started to smile.
   "Billy, that's great," she said. "What clever boys you both are."

Mom smiled at the dads too. "Come in and have some coffee," she said.

Billy and Rod raced each other and did
cartwheels over the grass.